The deadly setup

Acknowledgements

Cover design: Oliver Heath, Rafters Design

Illustrations on pages 17, 23 and 33 © Paul Gardiner, 2005. The right of Paul Gardiner to be identified as the illustrator of this work has been asserted by him in accordance with the Copyright, Design and Patents Act, 1988.

Brinsford books are a direct result of the findings of a two-year authoring/research project with young offenders at HMYOI Brinsford, near Wolverhampton. Grateful thanks go to all the young people who participated so enthusiastically in the project and to Judy Jackson and Brian Eccleshall of Dudley College of Technology.

First published in Great Britain by Axis Education Ltd

ISBN 1-84618-005-8

Axis Education PO Box 459
Shrewsbury SY4 4WZ

Email: enquiries@axiseducation.co.uk

www.axiseducation.co.uk

Chapter One

"God, I hope I've made the right choice," Pete mumbled to himself as he opened the door of the restaurant.

It was his dream. His first restaurant. He was sweating with nerves. Would he make enough money to pay back the bank loan?

Pete peered into the dull room. The windows were boarded up. Rays of light shining through the cracks turned into rays of dust.

He took a step further into the room and was swamped by a rotten smell.

"I need fresh air," he gasped. He heaved his size 12 Doc Marten boots at the wooden boards. With one kick they shattered and he yanked open the metal frame of the window. Welcome fresh air flooded the room. The remaining five windows got the same treatment.

Sunlight bounced off a metallic sign on a door at the back. 'Staff Only' it said. He hesitated before opening the door to the kitchen. How much work would he need to do here? He pushed at the door, expecting it to resist, or at least to creak. But it glided open as smoothly as if the hinges had just been oiled.

"I wish," Pete laughed to himself. He rolled up his sleeves ready for the huge job ahead of him. And then he gasped. The kitchen was in perfect order. Everything was just exactly where it should be. Except that it was covered with a thick layer of ageing dust.

"What a shame it all has to go," thought Pete. "If it wasn't so out of date I could have saved a fortune."

He started to collect up all the old kitchen equipment. Outside the back door was the yellow JCB skip he had hired yesterday, ready for the biggest spring clean of his life.

He must have made over a hundred trips to the skip by the time he left the restaurant that evening. He was tired and he ached all over. But his first day was done. The restaurant was cleared.

Tomorrow the cleaners would be in, and next week the painters would come and start to turn his dream into reality. If all went to plan it shouldn't take more than five or six weeks before he could get his new kit in. Then he would hire staff to make it all work. He began to plan the adverts in his head.

Exactly five weeks later, to the day, the kitchen was ready for its new gear. He couldn't believe how well it had all gone. He had even advertised for staff, he was so confident. The interviews would start tomorrow. Then it would be all systems go. He couldn't wait!

He couldn't sleep either. Not until about four in the morning. And then he slept right through the alarm. When he did wake the sun was blazing through his curtains.

"Damn! I'm going to miss the delivery!" He raced to the restaurant. But the delivery van was still waiting.

"Thanks for hanging on," said Pete.

"No worries. I just needed to make sure I was at the right place."

"What do you mean? The number's pretty clear on the door."

"You've already got a kitchen full back there."

Pete was puzzled. He followed the delivery man to the back door. He looked through the window that he had washed yesterday.

Stainless steel equipment gleamed in the light. The canopies, splash-backs and ovens. Even the sinks were spotless.

Pete blinked hard in disbelief. "What are you playing at, mate? This isn't the new stuff I ordered. It's all second-hand. I mean it's good quality, but I've paid for new stuff."

"Most of your order is still in the van, mate. I don't know anything about this lot."

There was something familiar about it. Over there – that was where the sinks had been. And he remembered those canopies.

Someone, or something, had cleaned up the old kitchen stuff and put everything back into its place.

Pete walked slowly round the kitchen and inspected it.

Maybe he didn't really need the new stuff after all.

It would save him about thirty thousand quid. He made up his mind.

"Sorry, but you've had a wasted journey," he told the driver. "I'm going to send the new stuff back."

Time enough to wonder why ...

But as the van drove off Pete had a fluttering feeling in his stomach. Had he made the right decision? Still, there was no going back now. There wasn't time. He had his first interviews in thirty minutes.

Chapter Two

Opening night arrived. It had been worth it. The doors would open at 7 pm. Would anyone turn up? He had spent enough on advertising, but you could never be sure.

He paced his restaurant. The thick blue carpet felt soft underfoot. The tables were laid with crisp white tablecloths, crystal glasses and silver cutlery. Fresh roses and damask cotton napkins completed the look. The restaurant looked like the bistro of his dreams – homely, but modern.

And the menu was fantastic. It should be. Adrian, the new chef, had cost him a packet. His last job had been at Brown's in London and he was good. Very good. At 32 he had already worked in three top London restaurants. Pete was lucky to have got him.

The clock struck seven and Pete unlocked the front doors.

His first customers did not arrive until an hour later. By this time beads of sweat had begun to appear on Pete's forehead. A young couple in their twenties sat at a table for two by the window. Jane served them expertly. He was glad he had chosen her and Phil over the others.

"I'm in business," Pete smiled to himself.

Over the next hour three more tables were taken. Phil and Jane shared the work between them.

Most of the diners had reached the dessert stage when the bell over the door rang again. A lone priest walked into the restaurant and stooped nervously by the front desk.

"A table for one, please."

Pete showed him to his table and handed him a menu. "Jane will come and take your order in a few minutes. Can I get you a drink?"

The priest grabbed Pete's hand tightly. "No. I need a word first."

Pete pulled his hand away and frowned.

"Please," begged the priest. "It's important. Can you sit down for a moment?"

"I can't right now, but I'll see you before you leave."

Pete went into the kitchen. "There's a loony guy out there – that one, the priest, on his own."

"What's wrong with him?" asked Jane.

Pete shrugged. "Dunno. He wants to talk to me. I said I'd see him later."

"Maybe he hasn't got any money," giggled Jane, and went out to serve her customers.

By the time Pete went back into the restaurant the priest was the only customer left.

Pete had rather hoped he would have left by now. The priest's presence made him feel oddly tense.

"You've not been open long, have you?" said the priest.

"First night tonight," said Pete.

"I'm sorry if I startled you earlier," said the priest. "How are things going?"

"Sorry, I didn't catch your name."

"Father Jones. I'm Father Dennis Jones. How are things around here?"

What's it to you? thought Pete. But the man was a customer. He had to be polite.

"Fine, thanks," he said easily. "Why do you ask?"

"I knew the last owners quite well."

"That must have been some time ago. What does it have to do with me? There isn't a body up the chimney or something, is there?" Pete laughed at his own joke but a strange shiver ran up his spine.

"Nothing. Nothing at all, really. It's just ... It's just that they had a few troubles and I helped them out. Look, I've really got to go now. If you ever need any help, here's my card."

And he left. Pete was baffled. But he had a lot to do still. He was still clearing vases when Jane and Adrian left.

"Night, both. Thanks for your hard work tonight. It was a good start."

Meanwhile, in the kitchen, Phil was doing the last of the washing up. He'd put all the pans and pots away and was carefully drying the chef's knives. They were razor sharp. He had already had a run in with a vegetable knife at the last place he had worked, so he was being doubly careful. Gingerly he put the knives back in their block and placed the meat cleaver back on its hook. As he picked up his denim jacket from the coat hook he heard the clank of metal behind him.

He turned, expecting to see Pete.

A strange whistling sound filled his ears.

"What the hell ...?"

Flashes of light reflected off whirling metal in front of his eyes.

Something crashed violently into his head. He opened his mouth to screech. No sound came. A terrible searing pain filled his head as the meat cleaver split through his skull.

Blood spattered over the freshly wiped surfaces, making a horrific mess. Ruby chunks of brains and flesh speckled the floor.

Phil's lifeless body hit the floor with a dull bounce. His skull split in two in a gruesome grin.

Chapter Three

In the next room Pete was startled by the noise. Perhaps it was the priest who had made him suspicious. It was probably only Phil dropping something. Even so, he went to the door armed with a Hoover pipe.

Fearfully, he pushed the swing doors open. And saw ...

Nothing.

He laughed to himself. Nothing but a sparkling kitchen. Phil's jacket had gone. He must have left by the back door. "That explains the thud," he said aloud.

It had been a great start, but now he was really whacked.

"Sod it, the hoovering can wait until morning," he thought.

Next day he arrived at the restaurant early. He spent most of the day on paperwork but still made it by five in the afternoon. Plenty of time to get the cleaning done before his staff arrived.

He put the radio on and began to hoover. The restaurant was due to open at seven. He'd check the kitchens and put in some fresh flowers.

He didn't realise that Jane had already turned up, early.

Last night the salads had run out, and Jane had been in a rush trying to prepare more while serving customers. Today she had decided to come in early to get the salads ready well in advance.

She took the vegetables out of the fridge and began her work.

There was only one small salad spinner. She made a mental note to ask Pete if he could buy something to speed along the process. As she lifted handfuls of greenery out of the sink she knocked a tomato into the plughole.

"Damn!" The plughole was also a waste disposal unit. But it didn't work. Pete had promised to get it fixed.

Jane rolled up her sleeves and reached down the hole to fish out the runaway tomato. She felt the cool metal. The rubbery skin of the tomato was just out of her reach. She stood on tiptoe and leaned further into the sink. She could feel the sharp chrome blades of the disposal unit on either side of the pipe.

A whirring noise made her jump. The motor of the disposal unit sprang into life. Metal blades flashed and spun. Jane tried to yank her hands away. The hairs on the back of her neck stood on end. Something was forcing her slender arm down the hole ...

"No!" The shout came out as a tortured whisper. The spinning blades sliced off Jane's delicate fingertips. The crunch of crushing bones and mashing flesh filled her ears. She let out a spine-tingling scream.

The blades whirred in rhythm with the music next door. In a matter of seconds her ordeal was over. The waste disposal unit sucked the last of Jane into its grinding jaws. Her flat black shoes were the only things that remained. Along with the spatters of blood and gristle in the sink.

17

Chapter Four

It was coming up for six o'clock when Pete came into the kitchen.

"Where the hell is everyone?" he shouted.

There was no sign of Jane. The mess in the sink had been cleared away, along with her shoes. Not a trace was left behind.

The back door was flung open. It was Adrian.

"I was wondering where you'd all got to," said a relieved Pete.

Adrian put on his apron and set about preparing the meats and sauces. "They'll be along soon," he said comfortably.

But half an hour later no waiting staff had turned up. Pete was annoyed. Jane and Phil should have been reliable. Their references were very good. Too good, perhaps?

Maybe he'd been taken for a ride. Now he had a long night waiting at tables ahead of him.

"Just wait till I see Jane and Phil ..."

It was a good night. Business was already starting to grow. He had had full tables for the first two hours. But it had been exhausting, with only Adrian in the kitchen and himself to wait on the tables. Not for the first time, he cursed Jane and Phil for not turning up, and for not even bothering to tell him. First call tomorrow would be to the job agency to get some more staff.

"Leave it, Adrian," he said wearily when the chef brought in the hoover to help him clean the floor. "We'll do all that in the morning. Thanks, mate. See you tomorrow."

It was early, too early for the agencies to be open, but he wanted to have his restaurant looking good. He put some music on to make the mundane task of mopping and vacuuming more bearable. After about thirty minutes he could hear a thumping noise over the bass line of the music. He turned down the volume.

The thumping began again. Someone knocking at the door. At this hour? Had he left his car lights on or something?

"Who is it?" Pete shouted as he walked over to the front door.

"Police. We'd like a word."

"Yeah, yeah. Hang on a minute." Pete tugged at the bolts on the front door. Finally he got them open. "Can I help you?"

"Just a few enquiries, sir." The taller of the two police officers elbowed his way in.

Why did he feel that little edge of cold fear? His drinks licence was all in order. He hadn't made a lot of noise – surely nobody could complain about ...

"We're investigating a couple of missing persons," said the tall officer.

"Missing ...? Sorry, but I think you must have come to the wrong place."

"I don't think so, sir." This was the shorter one. He took out a notebook. "Jane Green and Philip Davidson. They're both employed by you, I believe?"

"They were. But Phil and Jane didn't turn up for work yesterday. If you can tell me what's happened to them I'd like to know. I'm having to do my own table waiting, and ..."

After several more questions Pete began to feel his temper rising. The tone of the officers was distinctly unfriendly. Did they think he'd locked them up in a freezer or something? By the time the police left he was in a foul mood. Especially when he went to the job agency and there was simply no staff to be had. It was going to be another hard night.

He had never felt so glad when nine o'clock came and there were no more customers. He decided to call it a night. He told Adrian to pack up and began ringing up the till.

Adrian was washing up in the kitchen. When he'd finished the dishes he mopped the floor and sat on the counter for a breather. It wasn't often he got an early night. He decided to see if there was a late film on at the cinema.

He picked up the evening paper and checked out the details. There was a film he and his partner Steve had wanted to see for ages. "Great! Just time to pick him up and get there in time for the main feature."

He jumped off the counter in a rush. His feet slipped as they hit the wet floor. He tried to grab the counter top for support but only managed to grasp the dishcloth. The knife block had been resting on the dishcloth. It flew up into the air as Adrian slipped to the floor.

The knives soared out of the block. They seemed to spin in mid air. The block was the first thing to hit him. It landed square on his forehead and knocked him out cold. The knives followed very closely behind. They stabbed in quick succession.

If Adrian had been conscious he would have heard a sound familiar to all chefs – the sharpest of knives slicing into raw flesh. Then there was the gurgling of hot blood as it hit the cool air.

Chapter Five

Pete stumbled blearily out of bed. He had stayed up half the night finishing the cleaning. Boy, did he pick his staff! He couldn't believe they'd all just walked out on him. They'd seemed reliable when he'd taken them on. And the police seemed so suspicious. Strange that his staff seemed to vanish one by one ...

Pete shook himself. Enough. He couldn't afford silly thoughts like that. He'd get over to the restaurant and start phoning round more agencies to get staff. He wouldn't be able to open tonight. He'd never find the staff in time. His bank manager would go ape.

Pete shook himself again. A quick shower, coffee and then the restaurant. He must get on with things. This was what being in charge was really like.

As he opened the door to the restaurant Pete smiled. The phone was ringing. More bookings, he thought as he picked it up. Persuade them to wait a day or two, then it would be all systems go again ...

"Hello? Is that the restaurant? I'm Steve, Adrian's partner. Is he with you? I've been calling for hours but there's been no answer. Why hasn't he come home? Was he working late? He's not usually so thoughtless ..." The voice stopped to take breath.

"Steve – did you say that's your name? – I'm Pete, the owner. Sorry, but I can't help you. Adrian took off last night without even saying goodbye. I was a bit annoyed. There was a lot to discuss. I've been having staff problems, and I didn't think Adrian would mess me about. Not someone as good as him. I thought he must have a hot date. I've no idea where he went. He never said anything to me."

"What do you mean, a hot date? We live together." The voice sounded as if it would cry at any moment. "Our dates are each other. He's ultra-reliable. What have you done with him? I'm coming down to see for myself."

The phone went dead.

Pete shrugged. What did Steve think he was doing? Killing his staff one by one?

He could feel that cold shiver he'd had before, and the hairs at the back of his neck began to prickle.

Got to get on. He reached for the phone book to start hitting the agencies.

Pete had been phoning for a few minutes when the restaurant door opened. A guy in his late twenties with massive muscles walked through it. Pete finished his call – another agency with no one available. He'd definitely have to stay shut tonight. "Sorry about that. I'm trying to find replacement staff."

"I'm Darren. Jane Green's boyfriend. What the hell's going on? The police say Jane's not the only one gone missing. Another waiter's gone as well. Were they having some sort of thing together or what? But she'd never leave the kids. Have you searched this place properly?" Darren stopped for breath.

The door burst open again and a really skinny guy shot through it. "Have you found him yet? Have you found my Adrian? What sort of place is this?"

Pete broke in. "I've had just about enough of this. From both of you. Your respective partners have legged it, leaving me in the shit. Now go away. I have a restaurant to run. If I can find anyone to help me run it."

Darren looked at Steve. "You too?"

"Adrian. The best chef in the world. The best guy ..." He broke down into sobs.

"Three of them!" Darren said. "All three of them. One by one." He turned to Steve. "Come on. We're going to the police. This can't be a coincidence. Well, can it? Come on. I don't think this one's a hundred per cent safe."

The door banged shut behind them.

Pete sat with his head in his hands. Then he sat up suddenly. The attic! He had never been up in the attic. Maybe they were all in there, hiding. Maybe it was just some stupid prank they were playing. In his heart he knew that wasn't true. But he had to look. He grabbed the torch from under the counter by the till and began slowly to climb the stairs.

He opened the hatch and switched on the torch.

The attic was full of dust and cobwebs. Nothing else. Not even a footprint. Pete's stomach lurched with disappointment. He had clung to the hope that it was going to turn out to be a joke. He shuddered as the torch picked out a large trunk, the only thing in the entire space.

Curiosity got the better of him. The torch beam wavered as he clambered into the loft. He carefully opened the trunk lid.

There was nobody in there. The blind relief was mixed with another feeling. Where in hell were they?

He shone the torch onto the bits of paper at the bottom of the trunk.

Then he jumped.

They were newspaper clippings. About the restaurant. Pete knelt down and started to read.

Chapter Six

The first clipping shook Pete.

> *"Restaurant owner charged with killing.*
> *Police solve missing persons case."*

Pete read on. It was almost the same as had been happening to him. Staff had vanished. Police had investigated. No bodies were found but the restaurant owner had been sent to prison for murder.

He read on. The restaurant owner told his story. He had claimed that ghostly things had been going on. Pete thought back to the equipment that had magically reappeared in the kitchen, and shuddered. What could he do?

Then he remembered. The old priest. He started hunting through his pockets. The priest had given him a card. He had to find it.

He found the crumpled white card among a sheaf of receipts. He knew what he had to do. He bolted back down the hatch and rushed downstairs towards the front door. He heard the click of a key turning in the lock.

"Hello? Who's there?" His voice trembled. He tried to unlock the front door but his key didn't seem to fit.

Then terror struck him. "Let me out, you bastard! I've done nothing to you. Nothing!"

Out of the corner of his eye Pete caught a glimpse of something flying towards him.

He ducked. Something hit the door just behind him with a twang. He turned to see an enormous kitchen knife sticking out of the door.

"Oh, my God!" screamed Pete. "It's trying to kill me! I'm next!"

He dived behind a table and sat underneath it. How could he make his escape? He racked his brains. He could feel panic rise. Then he thought. The alarm! If he could only manage to set it, the sensors would seek him out and it would go off.

Pete glanced around. The knife had disappeared from the door. Shit! Still, he had to go for it, no matter what.

He leapt up and punched in the code for the alarm. He waited five long seconds for it to accept the code. A whooshing noise filled his ears. He ducked, but the knife clipped his sleeve. He gasped. The knife had nicked his arm and blood was seeping from a long thin cut. He ran across the room and hid behind the table again.

The alarm sounded. It sent a piercing pain through his head. Wasn't anybody going to do anything? Phone the police, you bastards out there! Don't just ignore it, do something!

It must have been only about five or six minutes, but it felt like a lifetime. He had never been so glad to hear police sirens in his life. He even welcomed the noise of splintering wood as they broke in to the restaurant.

"Thank you so much," he gushed. They'd never believe it about the knife. "I couldn't find my keys after I'd set the alarm ... Panicked a bit ..."

The sergeant cast his eyes around the room. "These keys here, sir?"

Pete was so relieved to be out of immediate danger that he didn't notice the sergeant's dry tone. "Thank you. Yes. Well, you see, I think there's a ghost here. He's been here before." Pete brandished the cuttings in the sergeant's face. "Look, thanks for your trouble. I can see you must be busy. Goodnight."

They didn't make much of a secret of the fact they thought he was stark, raving mad. Needing a plain van, not the police variety. But Pete didn't have time to notice their disbelieving expressions. He left for his flat. He needed to sort this out once and for all.

Chapter Seven

His hand shook as he dialled the old priest's number.

"Father Jones? It's Pete Farrow – from the restaurant. I'm in trouble. I need help."

He heard a heavy sigh from the end of the wire. "I rather thought you would. Give me your address. I'll come straight round."

Pete was so relieved when the old man arrived that he hugged him. Somehow he felt that the old man could help him. That he would believe him. Above all he needed someone to talk to.

As he reached the end of his story Pete sighed. He felt stupid now that he'd put the whole thing into words. How could anyone believe him? He looked fearfully at the priest who smiled at him reassuringly.

"I told you I knew the last owner of the restaurant. The same thing happened to him. There is some sort of evil being who is in control of the restaurant. I know it seems dramatic, but I think the only solution is to perform an exorcism. I offered to do it for the previous owner but he just refused. He couldn't believe that there was a supernatural cause for what was happening. Even after he was sent down for the murders he just couldn't accept the fact."

"Oh, thank God you believe me! It's such a relief. Please do the exorcism. Please. I can't stand much more of this. It's driving me crazy. Apart from anything else, where are Phil, Jane and Adrian? I'm really worried about them. Even though I only knew them for a short while, I feel kind of responsible for them. After all, I started it all up again by opening the restaurant."

The old man looked serious. "If the Presence that's here is operating the same way as it did before, I'm afraid they're probably dead. I'll have to see the bishop. We need permission to perform an exorcism. I'll also need some special equipment – an incense burner, some holy water and the special bible that we use. Meet me at the restaurant in the morning. I'm sure the bishop will agree, especially as the same things seem to be happening all over again."

Pete's stomach was tight with tension when he arrived at the restaurant at eight. To his great relief the priest was there already, holding a bulging bag.

As the priest walked through the restaurant he swung the incense burner. The smell was cloying and the perfume went up Pete's nose. The next step was to sprinkle holy water over the whole restaurant. The old man chanted Latin from the heavy book.

There was a rush of noise and shrieking. Doors slammed and opened again. The mirror shattered and glass showered all over the restaurant, way beyond where the glass should have fallen. Pete's forehead was gashed and blood started to drip steadily.

The silence which followed was like the aftermath of a bomb. Pete and Father Jones looked at each other.

It was over. He was free.

Chapter Eight

The restaurant slowly returned to normal. Pete started to feel in control again. Business had really taken off. Things were better than ever. Profits were up, the bank manager was happy and the new staff were working out fine. Pete tried not to think about the evil spirit and its terrifying work. When he did, by accident, it seemed more and more unreal.

It was about three months later. The first customers of the evening were scanning their menus. Pete was in the kitchen talking to one of his newer waiters. He heard some fuss in the restaurant and the swing doors to the kitchen burst open. Three police officers barged in.

The senior officer approached him. "Pete Farrow?"
"Excuse me, officers, but this is a working kitchen. Would you like to come into my office?"

Conscious of his staff's eyes staring at him, he took them into the cubby hole he called his office. "Can I help you?"

The senior officer met his eyes. "Peter Farrow, I am arresting you on suspicion of the murders of Phil Davidson, Jane Green and Adrian Burgess. You do not have to ..."

Pete cut in. "Are you fucking insane? How can you accuse me of that? I haven't done any murders! I'm too busy. Can't you see I've got a restaurant to run?"

"We have evidence," said the officer woodenly.

"Evidence? What evidence?" he stuttered in angry disbelief.

"DNA and plenty of fingerprints to link you with the murders. We found the bodies where you stashed them in Honour Woods."

The police handcuffed Pete and dragged him towards the restaurant door. Heads turned, mouths dropped open.

An echo rang in his head. "I told you I'd get you in the end."

A hollow laugh filled Pete's ears.

"Can't you hear that?" he shrieked. "Any of you? It wasn't me! Listen. The voice is laughing. It's him. It's not me. I tell you, I didn't do it! It's him ..."